THE QUANTUM MECHANICS OF VOODOO

BRYCE MATTHEWS

THE QUANTUM MECHANICS OF VOODOO

ROYCE
MATTHEWS

Dear Reader,

Thank you for purchasing The Quantum Mechanics of Voodoo. I hope that this book has provided you with a new perspective on the world, and that it has helped you understand the principles of quantum mechanics and voodoo in a new and exciting way.

Writing this book has been a journey of discovery for me, and I'm honored that you have chosen to join me on this journey. I hope that the information and exercises in this book have been helpful and have had a positive impact on your life.

I would love to hear about your experience reading our book. Your feedback is important to me and helps me improve my future work. Please don't hesitate to reach out to me and share your thoughts, insights, and any other feedback you might have.

Thank you again for your support and I wish you all the best on your personal growth journey.

Sincerely,

Royce Matthews

ceux qui ont acheté ce livre seront récompensés par la prospérité, mais rappelez-vous toujours que la douleur est tout aussi importante que la joie.

PROLOGUE

In the world of science, quantum mechanics has been revolutionizing our understanding of the universe. It has shown us that the world is not as simple and straightforward as we once thought. It has revealed that the universe is full of mysteries and wonders that are yet to be explored.

On the other hand, voodoo is a traditional African religion that has been practiced for centuries. It has been misunderstood and misrepresented in popular culture, being portrayed as a form of evil magic or black magic.

But what if we could combine the principles of quantum mechanics and voodoo? What if we could unlock the power of the universe and use it to change our lives for the better?

This is the premise of this book, The Quantum Mechanics of Voodoo. It is a journey into the unknown, where science and spirituality meet. It is a guide to understanding the principles of quantum mechanics and voodoo, and how they can be applied to personal growth and development.

This book is not only for those who are interested in science and spirituality, but also for anyone who is looking for a new way of understanding the world and themselves. It is for anyone who wants to unlock the power of the universe and use it to create change in their lives.

Are you ready to embark on this journey? Are you ready to discover the quantum mechanics of voodoo?

Let's begin

Chapter 1

VOODOO AND OTHER SPIRITUALITIES: MISUNDERSTOOD AND MISREPRESENTED

Voodoo, also known as Vodou or Vodun, is a traditional African religion that has been practiced for centuries. However, it has often been misrepresented and misunderstood in popular culture, being portrayed as a form of evil magic or black magic. The same can be said for many other spiritualities and religions that have been deemed as "evil" or "negative" by society.

The origins of voodoo can be traced back to West Africa, where it was practiced by the Fon, Yoruba, and Kongo peoples. The religion was brought to the Caribbean and the Americas during the transatlantic slave trade, where it evolved and blended with other traditions and beliefs.

Voodoo, like any other religion, is based on a set of beliefs, rituals, and practices that are meant to connect individuals with the spiritual realm. It is not a form of evil magic or black magic, but rather a way of understanding and interacting with the world.

The misconception of voodoo being evil or negative can be attributed to several factors. One of them is the lack of understanding and knowledge about the religion. Another is the tendency of society to demonize and stereotype anything that is different or unfamiliar.

This is not only limited to voodoo, but also to many other spiritualities and religions that have been wrongly deemed as "evil" or "negative" by society. This is because of the lack of understanding and knowledge, and the tendency of society to demonize and stereotype anything that is different or unfamiliar.

It is important to remember that every religion and spirituality has its own set of beliefs, practices and rituals, and it is not fair to judge or stereotype them based on lack of knowledge or understanding. It is important to respect and understand different spiritualities and religions, and to avoid spreading misinformation and stereotypes.

In conclusion, Voodoo and other spiritualities have been wrongly deemed as evil or negative, this is due to lack of knowledge and understanding, and the tendency of society to demonize and stereotype anything that is different or unfamiliar. It is important to respect and understand different spiritualities and religions and avoid spreading misinformation and stereotypes

Chapter 2

THE ORIGINS OF VOODOO: THE OLDEST RELIGION AND OCCUPATION

Voodoo, also known as Vodou or Vodun, is often considered to be one of the oldest religions in the world. It has its roots in West Africa, where it was practiced by the Fon, Yoruba, and Kongo peoples. The religion was brought to the Caribbean and the Americas during the transatlantic slave trade, where it evolved and blended with other traditions and beliefs.

Voodoo is considered to be one of the oldest religions in the world because of its deep roots in West African culture and spirituality. The origins of voodoo can be traced back to the ancient kingdoms of West Africa, where it was a way of understanding and interacting with the world. The religion was passed down through generations by oral tradition, and it has been an important part of West African culture for centuries.

But voodoo is not only one of the oldest religions, it is also one of the oldest occupations, it was considered as a way of healing, divination and communication with the spiritual realm. The practitioners of voodoo, also known as "Houngans" or "Mambos", were respected members of the community and played an important role in the social, cultural, and spiritual life of the people.

Voodoo was not only a way of understanding the world, but also a way of healing and divination. The Houngans and Mambos were healers, diviners, and spiritual leaders who were respected and valued members of the community. They were able to heal physical and emotional illnesses, provide guidance and advice, and help people connect with the spiritual realm.

However, the religion has been misrepresented and misunderstood in the modern world. With the slave trade, voodoo was brought to the Caribbean and the Americas, where it was often suppressed, demonized and misrepresented. It was portrayed as a form of evil magic or black magic, which led to a misunderstanding of the religion and its true nature.

It is important to remember that voodoo, like any other religion, is based on a set of beliefs, rituals, and practices that are meant to connect individuals with the spiritual realm. It is not a form of evil magic or black magic, but rather a way of understanding and interacting with the world. It is also important to remember that voodoo has been one of the oldest religion and occupation, and it has played an important role in the history and culture of many societies.

In conclusion, voodoo is one of the oldest religions and oldest occupation in the world, and it has deep roots in West African culture and spirituality. It has been passed down through generations by oral tradition and has been an important part of West African culture for centuries. It is important to remember that voodoo is not a form of evil magic or black magic but a way of understanding, healing and communicating with the spiritual realm. And it has played an important role in the history and culture of many societies.

Chapter 3
UNDERSTANDING QUANTUM PHYSICS

Quantum physics is the branch of physics that deals with the behavior of particles on a very small scale, such as atoms and subatomic particles. It is a fundamental theory in physics that has been developed over the past century and has led to many groundbreaking discoveries and technologies.

One of the key principles of quantum physics is that particles can exist in multiple states at the same time, a concept known as superposition. This means that an atom, for example, can exist in multiple energy levels at the same time, until it is observed or measured. This principle is also known as wave-particle duality.

Another important principle of quantum physics is the Heisenberg Uncertainty Principle, which states that it is impossible to know certain properties of a particle, such as its position and momentum, simultaneously with complete accuracy. This means that the more accurately we know the position of a particle, the less accurately we can know its momentum, and vice versa.

Quantum physics also introduced the concept of entanglement, which means that two particles can become connected in such a way that the state of one particle can affect the state of the other, no matter how far apart they are. This principle has been used to develop technologies such as quantum teleportation and quantum computing.

One of the most famous and counterintuitive theory in quantum physics is the Schrodinger's cat thought experiment, where a cat is placed inside a box with a radioactive atom, and a Geiger counter. According to quantum mechanics, the cat is both alive and dead until the box is opened, and the state of the cat is observed. This experiment illustrates the concept of superposition, and the collapse of the wave-function that occurs when a system is observed.

Quantum physics has led to many groundbreaking discoveries and technologies, such as transistors, lasers, and solar cells. It has also led to a better understanding of the nature of the universe, and has opened up new possibilities for research and experimentation.

In conclusion, quantum physics is the branch of physics that deals with the behavior of particles on a very small scale, such as atoms and subatomic particles. It introduces the principles of superposition, wave-particle duality, Heisenberg uncertainty principle, entanglement, and the collapse of the wave-function. These principles have led to many groundbreaking discoveries and technologies, and have opened up new possibilities for research and experimentation. It has also led to a better understanding of the nature of the universe.

Chapter 4

QUANTUM ENTANGLEMENT: THE MYSTERIOUS CONNECTION

Quantum entanglement is one of the most mysterious and fascinating principles of quantum physics. It is the phenomenon where two particles become connected in such a way that the state of one particle can affect the state of the other, no matter how far apart they are.

The concept of entanglement was first proposed by Albert Einstein, Boris Podolsky, and Nathan Rosen in 1935, in a paper called "Can Quantum-Mechanical Description of Physical Reality be Considered Complete?". They argued that the principles of quantum mechanics were not complete, and that there must be a hidden variable that explained the behavior of entangled particles.

However, it was later proven by physicist John Bell that there is no hidden variable and that the principles of quantum mechanics are indeed complete. This was done through a series of experiments known as Bell's Inequalities, which showed that the behavior of entangled particles cannot be explained by any hidden variable, and that the particles truly are connected in a mysterious way.

Entanglement is not just a theoretical concept; it has been observed in many experiments, such as the famous double-slit experiment, where the behavior of two entangled particles was observed to be correlated, even when the particles were separated by large distances.

Entanglement has many potential applications, such as quantum teleportation, quantum computing, and quantum cryptography. It also has implications for our understanding of the nature of the universe.

In conclusion, quantum entanglement is a mysterious and fascinating principle of quantum physics, it is the phenomenon where two particles become connected in such a way that the state of one particle can affect the state of the other, no matter how far apart they are. It was first proposed by Einstein, Podolsky and Rosen, and later proven by John Bell through a series of experiments. It has many potential applications and implications for our understanding of the nature of the universe.

Chapter 5

THE CORRELATIONS BETWEEN QUANTUM PHYSICS AND VOODOO: INTENT AND THE OBSERVER'S PERCEPTION

In the previous chapters, we have explored the principles of quantum physics and voodoo separately. However, it is important to note that there are many correlations and similarities between the two. One of the main similarities is the concept of intent and the observer's perception.

In quantum physics, it is well-established that the observer's perception plays a crucial role in the behavior of particles. The act of observation causes the collapse of the wave-function, which determines the state of a particle. This means that the observer's perception has the power to affect the behavior of particles on a subatomic level.

In voodoo, the concept of intent is also crucial. It is believed that one's thoughts and intentions have the power to affect the spiritual realm and bring about change in the physical world. The use of symbols, rituals, and spells is believed to be a way of focusing one's intent and directing it towards a specific goal.

Both quantum physics and voodoo also share the idea that the observer's perception and intent can affect the outcome of an event. In quantum physics, the observer's perception affects the behavior of particles, while in voodoo, the observer's intent affects the outcome of a ritual or spell.

Another correlation between the two is that both quantum physics and voodoo suggest that reality is not as fixed or objective as we may think, but rather it is shaped by our perception and intent.

In conclusion, there are many correlations and similarities between quantum physics and voodoo. One of the main similarities is the concept of intent and the observer's perception. Both suggest that reality is not as fixed or objective as we may think, but rather it is shaped by our perception and intent. Both quantum physics and voodoo propose that the observer's perception and intent can affect the outcome of an event.

Chapter 6

QUANTUM ENTANGLEMENT

Quantum entanglement is a phenomenon in quantum physics where two particles become connected in such a way that the state of one particle can instantaneously affect the state of the other particle, even if the two particles are separated by large distances. This phenomenon was first described by Albert Einstein, Boris Podolsky, and Nathan Rosen in 1935, and later by Erwin Schrödinger in 1935, who coined the term "entanglement."

The Basics of Quantum Entanglement

In quantum physics, particles can exist in multiple states simultaneously, known as superposition. When two particles become entangled, their states become linked, and the state of one particle will affect the state of the other particle, regardless of the distance between them. This is known as non-local correlation.

An example of quantum entanglement is the famous "double-slit experiment." In this experiment, a beam of particles is shot at a screen with two slits, creating an interference pattern on a detector screen behind it. When the particles are entangled, the interference pattern remains the same, even when one of the particles is measured, indicating that the state of one particle is affecting the state of the other particle.

Entanglement and Communication

Quantum entanglement has the potential to revolutionize the field of communication. Because the state of one particle can affect the state of another particle, regardless of the distance between them, entangled particles can be used to transmit information faster than the speed of light. This is known as quantum teleportation.

However, it's important to note that quantum entanglement is not a way to send information faster than light, but a way to describe the correlation between particles and how the state of one particle affects the state of another.

Entanglement in Real World Applications

Quantum entanglement has the potential to be used in a variety of real-world applications, such as in quantum computing and cryptography. In quantum computing, entangled particles can be used to perform calculations much faster than traditional computers. In cryptography, entangled particles can be used to create unbreakable codes.

Conclusion

In conclusion, quantum entanglement is a fascinating phenomenon in quantum physics that has the potential to revolutionize the field of communication and technology. Further research is needed to fully understand and harness the power of entanglement.

Chapter 7
VOODOO DOLLS

Voodoo dolls are a form of folk magic that is associated with the religion of Voodoo, which is practiced mainly in Haiti and other parts of the Caribbean. The dolls are believed to be a way to represent a person or a spirit and to exert control over them through various rituals and practices.

Origins and History

The origins of voodoo dolls can be traced back to the religion of Voodoo, which was brought to the Caribbean by enslaved West Africans. The dolls were believed to be a representation of the Loa, or spirits, that were worshipped in the religion. They were used in rituals and ceremonies as a way to connect with and invoke the spirits.

The Use of Voodoo Dolls

Voodoo dolls are used in a variety of rituals and practices, such as healing, protection, and curse-breaking. They are also used to represent a person or a spirit and to exert control over them through various rituals and practices. For example, a voodoo doll may be used to bring good luck or to curse an enemy.

Making a Voodoo Doll

Voodoo dolls are typically made from materials such as cloth, wax, or wood, and are often decorated with beads, shells, and other decorative items. They can be made to represent a specific person or spirit, and may be made to look like the person they are meant to represent.

It's important to note that voodoo doll use is considered as a negative practice, it's not something that should be done without the consent of the person being represented, and it's not something that should be taken lightly. Misuse of voodoo dolls can have serious consequences and it's not something that should be done without proper understanding of the culture and the spirituality behind it.

Conclusion

In conclusion, voodoo dolls are a form of folk magic that is associated with the religion of Voodoo, which is practiced mainly in Haiti and other parts of the Caribbean. They are believed to be a way to represent a person or a spirit and to exert control over them through various rituals and practices. It's important to have a cultural and spiritual understanding of the practice before attempting to make or use voodoo dolls, and to always have the consent of the person being represented.

Chapter 8

THE CORRELATIONS OF VOODOO DOLLS AND QUANTUM ENTANGLEMENT

Many people might not see the correlation between quantum entanglement and voodoo dolls, but there are actually many similarities. In order for a voodoo doll to work, it is said that you need a piece of clothing or DNA from the person that the doll represents. Similarly, in quantum entanglement, you can use two DNA strands and manipulate one, and the other DNA will be affected. This is much like how voodoo dolls work. When someone uses a voodoo doll, they use their intent and a person's DNA or an article of clothing to manipulate the person that the doll represents. By manipulating the doll, it is believed that the person's life can be affected. However, it is important to remember that by doing this, you will also keep yourself tormented. We are all connected, and you cannot hurt someone or come with ill intent without expecting a backlash from the spiritual world.

Witchcraft and the belief in the power of certain objects and talismans is a widespread belief across many cultures. Some people believe that these objects can be harmful and will hire a "witchcraft removal expert" or an exorcist to remove them safely. Some people also believe that witchcraft can be used to possess a person with demons. There is a belief that certain objects can perform actions at a distance, similar to the concept of quantum entanglement in physics, where two objects remain connected even after being separated by vast distances. However, there is no scientific basis for the claim that these objects can perform such actions.

It is important to note that these beliefs are not supported by scientific evidence and should not be taken as fact. Many of these beliefs have cultural and historical roots and have been passed down through generations. It is up to each individual to decide what they believe about these concepts.

Chapter 9

WITCHCRAFT IS NOT VOODOO

Witchcraft and Voodoo are two distinct spiritual practices that have been misunderstood and misrepresented throughout history.

Witchcraft, also known as Wicca, is a modern pagan, witchcraft religion that can be traced back to the early 20th century. It is based on the worship of nature and the veneration of a goddess and god as representative of the feminine and masculine aspects of the universe. Wiccans follow a moral code known as the Wiccan Rede, which states "An ye harm none, do what ye will." They also practice magic, which is understood as the manipulation of natural energy to bring about desired change.

Voodoo, on the other hand, is an Afro-Caribbean religion that originated in West Africa and was brought to the Caribbean and the Americas through the transatlantic slave trade. It is based on the worship of spirits known as Loa and the belief in a supreme creator god. Voodoo practitioners also believe in the power of magic and the use of charms and rituals to bring a bout change. However, unlike Wicca, Voodoo also includes the use of possession by the spirits, and it's sometimes also called Vodou.

Both witchcraft and Voodoo have been the subject of much misinformation and stereotype, and both have been portrayed as dark and evil practices. This is not the case, both practices are peaceful and their practitioners are guided by their own moral code and the use of rituals and magic is to bring positive change in their lives and the lives of others.

It's important to note that neither of these practices should be feared or stigmatized, and that the beliefs and practices of these spiritual traditions should be respected and understood. It is also important to remember that the representation of these practices in popular culture is often sensationalized and bears little resemblance to their true nature.

Chapter 10
THE SERPENT

In Christianity, snakes are often associated with evil and deceit, as they are portrayed as the tempter in the story of Adam and Eve in the Bible. In the book of Genesis, a serpent tempts Eve to eat the forbidden fruit from the Tree of Knowledge, leading to the fall of man and the introduction of sin into the world. This portrayal of snakes as deceivers has been reinforced in other parts of the Bible, such as in the story of Moses and the Israelites in the wilderness, where a bronze serpent is used to heal those who have been bitten by venomous snakes.

In contrast, in Voodoo, snakes are often seen as powerful and benevolent spirits. They are believed to possess great wisdom and knowledge, and are sometimes called upon to provide guidance and protection. In Voodoo rituals, snakes are often invoked as spirits of healing and fertility, and are sometimes associated with the loa (Voodoo spirits) Damballah and Ayida Wedo.

It is important to note that the depiction of snakes in Christianity and Voodoo are cultural representation. In Christianity, the story of Adam and Eve is a symbolic representation of the human condition, the serpent represent the tempter, the one who tempt us to do something that is against the rule of God. In Voodoo, the snake is a representation of the powerful and benevolent spirits that can be invoked for help and guidance.

EPILOGUE

This book was created to suggests that modern physics is revealing that certain principles and beliefs that have traditionally been attributed to the spiritual realm also exist in the physical world. This could be detrimental to religion if faith is based solely on these principles or beliefs. However, it is suggested that this realization should not be used to dismantle the foundations of true mysticism, as the divine is beyond the realm of experimental science and cannot be experienced through it. Instead, the concept of spirituality should be redefined by acknowledging the physical nature of many spiritual manifestations, and by recognizing that matter is not an inferior, non-conscious element of the universe, but is intrinsically psychic.

ABOUT THE AUTHOR

Royce Matthews, hailing from St. Martinsville, Louisiana and raised in a strict Christian household, developed an interest in various religions and spiritual practices after moving to Georgia at the age of 12. His curiosity for the mystic and passion for science have always been a guiding force in his life.